PEGASUS AND THE PROUD PRINCE

and

The Flying Carpet

Retold by MARGARET MAYO
Illustrated by PETER BAILEY

ORCHARD BOOKS

For Natalie
M.M.
With love to the two young whippersnappers,
Oscar and Felix
P.B.

Orchard Books
96 Leonard Street, London EC2A 4XD
Orchard Books Australia
32/45-51 Huntley Street, Alexandria, NSW 2015
The text was first published in Great Britain in the form
of a gift collection called *The Orchard Book of Magical Tales*
and *The Orchard Book of Mythical Birds and Beasts*
illustrated by Jane Ray, in 1993 and 1996
This edition first published in hardback in 2003
First paperback publication in 2004

A CIP catalogue record for this book is available from the British Library
ISBN 1 84362 078 2 (hardback)
ISBN 1 84362 086 3 (paperback)
1 3 5 7 9 10 8 6 4 2 (hardback)
1 3 5 7 9 10 8 6 4 2 (paperback)
Printed in Great Britain

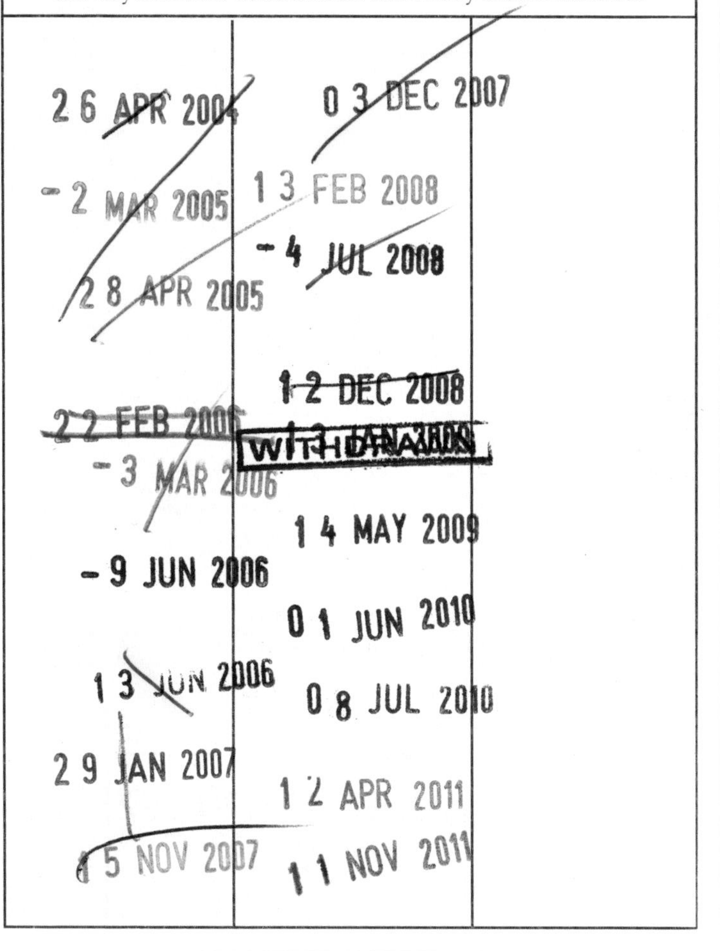
26 APR 2004
-2 MAR 2005
28 APR 2005
22 FEB 2006
-3 MAR 2006
-9 JUN 2006
13 JUN 2006
29 JAN 2007
15 NOV 2007
03 DEC 2007
13 FEB 2008
-4 JUL 2008
12 DEC 2008
WITHDRAWN
14 MAY 2009
01 JUN 2010
08 JUL 2010
12 APR 2011
11 NOV 2011

00 654574 00

CONTENTS

PEGASUS
AND THE PROUD PRINCE

Pegasus was a wild and beautiful snow-white horse who had huge feathered wings and could fly. He roamed freely about the land of Greece in the far-off times when gods lived on earth. No one had ever ridden him. No one had even got close enough to touch him, until a certain young prince learned the secret of how to tame this beautiful flying horse.

The prince's name was Bellerophon. He was, of course, a handsome, lively and daring prince, and he loved travel and adventure. But he was not perfect. Who is? Prince Bellerophon's trouble was that he thought rather a lot of himself, and reckoned he could do anything. In fact he was something of a show-off!

On his travels the prince heard about King Iobates, who ruled a country to the north of Greece called Lycia.

The king was rich, *and* he had a lovely daughter, *and* he had promised she would marry anyone who could kill a truly awful and ferocious three-headed monster that was rampaging around the country, breathing out fire and destroying everything.

'I shall go to Lycia,' Prince Bellerophon thought to himself. 'Straight away.' And he did.

When the prince arrived he was welcomed by King Iobates and invited to a feast where all the talk was about the three-headed monster. Nothing else. She was called the Chimera, and she really was weird-looking.

She had a lion's head at the front of her body, a goat's head growing out of the middle, while a long twisty snake was attached to the place where a tail should have been. She had lion's legs and claws, but the shaggy body of a goat. Most frightening of all, from each of her three mouths she blasted out fierce flames and vile-smelling poisonous fumes.

"Wherever she goes, she burns and destroys," said the king. "My bravest heroes have gone out to hunt her, but not one has returned. It's impossible to kill the Chimera!"

"There must be a way..." murmured Bellerophon, almost to himself. "It must be possible."

The king was annoyed. "So you, my fine prince, are going to rid us of the monster!" he said. "Good! Come back when you've done it!"

And Bellerophon, who was such a proud young man, looked straight at the king and said, “I shall try!”

That night Bellerophon lay awake trying to work out how he could kill the Chimera. ‘If only I could shoot at her with arrows, from above,’ he thought. ‘From just beyond the reach of her fierce flames and deadly breath. If only I could fly…’ And then he remembered Pegasus. “I must find the winged horse. Catch him and tame him.”

Now Bellerophon, like everyone else, believed that the winged horse belonged to the gods. So he took his bow and arrows, boarded a ship and sailed to Greece. When he arrived, he went to the temple of the goddess Athene and prayed for her help.

The prince was tired, so he lay down while he waited for a message from the goddess, and just before dawn he fell asleep. Then he dreamt that a slender woman, dressed in white, stood beside him. In her hands she held a horse's bridle made of gold. "Take this," she said. "With it you can tame Pegasus, who can be found by the enchanted pool which he made with one stamp of his hoof. The pool is high up on the mountain called Helicon."

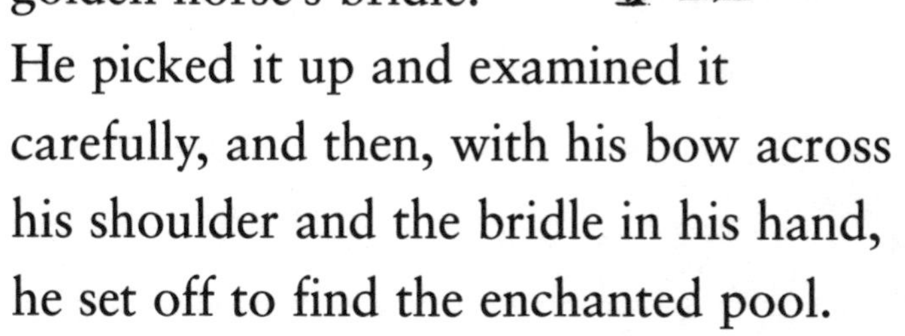

When the prince woke, he saw, lying on the floor beside him...a golden horse's bridle. He picked it up and examined it carefully, and then, with his bow across his shoulder and the bridle in his hand, he set off to find the enchanted pool.

He walked and walked. He came to the mountain and climbed the slopes, and at last he found a place where cool clear water bubbled up from underground into a pool that was shaped like a large horse's hoof.

Prince Bellerophon sat down, a little way off, resting his back against the trunk of a gnarled old olive tree. He waited, but Pegasus didn't come. It grew dark, and once again the prince fell asleep.

In the morning he was woken by the sound of great wings beating steadily. He looked up, and it seemed as if an enormous snow-white bird with glistening, silver-tipped wings was flying towards the mountain.

But this was not a bird. It was Pegasus.

The wingbeats grew slower, and the wonderful horse came gliding down and landed beside the pool. He folded his wings, lowered his beautiful snow-white head and began to drink.

Slowly the prince rose to his feet and with the bridle in his hands tiptoed towards Pegasus. The horse looked up, snorted loudly, stamped his hoofs and spread his wings ready to fly. But then he caught sight of the golden bridle. Immediately he folded his wings and waited, quiet as a lamb, until the prince came right up beside him and slipped the golden bit into his mouth.

The prince stroked the horse's long white mane and gently touched the silver-tipped wings. "Pegasus, greatest of horses," he said, "take me to Lycia and help me kill that dreadful monster the Chimera!"

The prince laid both his hands between the folded wings and jumped lightly on to the horse's back. When he was seated, he took hold of the golden reins. "Now fly!" he called out. And Pegasus spread his wings, slowly beat them up and down, and leaped into the air.

Up and up, they soared together, Pegasus flying faster and faster. How Prince Bellerophon enjoyed himself, riding high in the sky and looking down at the world below! "This," he said, "is the best and only way to travel!"

They flew on, and in a few hours they reached Lycia. At first the countryside below was full of colour, and alive with people and animals. There were fruit trees and vines growing on the hillsides, bright vegetable patches, wild flowers and fields of corn.

But before long they came to a place that was utterly destroyed by fire. The grass, the trees, every single plant was black. The houses were empty, burnt-out ruins. There were no men and women, no children, no animals. Everything was dead.

Still they flew on, looking for the Chimera, until Bellerophon saw smoke drifting out from the mouth of a cave. "That cave must be the Chimera's den," said the prince. "Fly down. Let's have a closer look."

Down swooped Pegasus, neighing loudly. And the Chimera heard, gave a long loud lion's roar and came padding out of the cave. When she saw Pegasus and the prince, she leaped towards them, spouting out long fierce flames and poisonous fumes from her three mouths. The heat was almost unbearable and the smell of the fumes was vile.

But Prince Bellerophon let go of the golden reins and, gripping hold of the horse with his knees, fixed an arrow in his bow, took aim, fired the arrow and struck the Chimera in her lion's throat. The monster roared and belched out more flames and fumes. The prince could hardly breathe, and that would have been the end of him, only the wonderful horse swiftly swerved sideways and flew upwards until they reached cool fresh air again.

When they had both recovered, the prince urged Pegasus to dive down once more into the smoke and flames. The prince took aim again, and this time he shot an arrow into the monster's heart. She stumbled and fell to the ground, writhing and rolling around, and roaring loudly in her pain and fury.

Then the horse and rider rose up again and hovered in the cool fresh air and waited. After a while the flames died down, the smoke began to clear, and they could see that the Chimera lay on the ground, quiet and still. She was dead.

The prince patted Pegasus fondly on the neck. “Wonderful horse,” he said, “our work is done, so take me now to King Iobates’s palace.” And he shook the golden reins and they were off, flying through the air.

When the prince returned to the palace with Pegasus, and told the king that they had killed the Chimera, there were, as you can imagine, lots of smiles, lots of congratulations and a big celebration feast. Everyone was so glad that the terrible Chimera was dead, and the rest of the country saved from destruction.

And then? Not long after, the handsome prince married the king's only daughter *and* he was made heir to the kingdom!

And of course he still had the golden bridle and often rode the wonderful horse Pegasus. So Prince Bellerophon was happy.

And that should have been the end of the story. But – remember – the prince thought rather a lot of himself to begin with and reckoned he could do anything. Well, as time went by, he became an even *bigger* show-off! He would say, "Who killed the Chimera? I did! Has anyone else a horse like mine? *No one!* I am…*just like the gods!*"

He couldn't stop thinking how amazingly clever and important he was, until one day he decided to visit the gods in their earthly home on Mount Olympus. So he placed the golden bridle on the horse, mounted, and told him to fly to Olympus.

Pegasus flew up into the air, higher and higher. He set his head towards Mount Olympus and flew on.

But the gods see everything. And Zeus, king of the gods, was angry. "So this proud young man thinks he is like a god," he said.

And he sent an insect with a very sharp sting, and it stung Pegasus, who was so surprised that he reared up and threw Prince Bellerophon off his back. And the prince fell down a long, long way to the ground – and he died.

But Pegasus continued his journey. When he finally reached Olympus, the gods welcomed him, and Zeus claimed the horse for his own special use.

"Pegasus," he said, "whenever I make storms in the sky, you shall carry the thunder and lightning bolts for me."

And, to this day, Pegasus works for Zeus. So, next time the thunder rolls and lightning flashes, look up, and if you are lucky you may catch a glimpse of Pegasus, the winged horse, flying across the sky.

A Greek tale

THE FLYING CARPET

There was once a prince who was so fond of hunting that he rode out every day in search of game. But one day he had no luck and by late afternoon had caught nothing. He rode on and on until he reached a dark jungle where he had never been before. There he came upon a flock of parrots, perched in amongst the trees, and he lifted his bow and took aim.

But before he could shoot, there was a whirl and flurry of feathers and the parrots flew up and away, leaving one bird still sitting there.

"Do not shoot me!" said the bird. "I am the raja of all parrots. I am the one that can tell you about Princess Maya."

The prince lowered his bow and rode up to the bird. "Princess Maya!" he said. "Who is Princess Maya?"

"Ahhh – the beautiful Princess Maya," said the parrot. "What can I say? She is radiant as the moon...warm and gentle as the evening sun. In this great world she is beyond compare."

"Where does she live?" asked the prince. "And how can I find her?"

"Go forward, ever forward," said the parrot, "through dark jungles and across wide plains, and you will find her."

Then the prince rode home, and on the way he made up his mind to find the beautiful Princess Maya, even if he had to search the whole world.

When he told his mother and father about the beautiful princess, they were sad. He was their only child, their golden treasure, and they did not want to lose him. But the prince had decided to go and he would not change his mind.

The very next morning he dressed in his finest clothes, took his bow and arrows and some food for the journey, mounted his favourite horse and set off.

Well, he rode until he reached the dark jungle where he had seen the parrots. And then he rode forward, ever forward. He crossed a wide plain, and still he rode forward. He entered a second, even darker jungle and, all of a sudden, he heard loud, angry voices; and in a clearing near by, he saw three demons – three small, sharp-eyed, wicked-looking demons – bunched round a small pile of things lying on the ground. There was a bag, a stick and an ancient carpet.

"What is the matter?" asked the prince.

One of the demons pointed to the things lying on the ground, "Our master died and left us these," he said, "and I want *all* of them!"

"And so do I!" shouted the second demon.

"Me too!" shrieked the third.

"A bag, a stick and an old carpet?" said the prince. "They're not worth quarrelling about!"

"*Not worth quarrelling about!*" The first demon squalled it out, fair cracked his throat. "Not worth quarrelling about! Why, the bag will give you anything you ask for. And the stick will beat your enemies and – see the rope coiled round it? – that will tie them up so they can't escape. As for the carpet…it will take you anywhere you want to go."

"Is that so?" said the prince. And he did some quick thinking. "Maybe I could help settle the quarrel," he suggested.

"I shall take three arrows and shoot them in the air, and the first one of you to find an arrow and bring it back can have all the treasures."

"Yes! yes!" the little demons agreed. Each one certain *he* was the fastest runner. Each one certain *he* would win.

So the prince let fly three arrows, and off they ran, full pelt.

And what next? The prince jumped down from his horse, turned it round to face the way they had come and said, "Lift your hooves, my fine horse, and gallop home!" And the horse galloped off.

The prince picked up the stick and the bag. He unrolled the carpet, sat down on it, crossed his legs and said, "Carpet! Take me to the city where Princess Maya lives!"

The carpet fluttered and then rose slowly upwards. When it was higher than the trees, it simply flew through the air. Smooth and steady, it flew and it flew, over dark jungles and wide plains. It flew and it

flew, until it came to the edge of a great city. Then it gently floated downwards.

As soon as the carpet touched the ground, the prince stood up, stretched himself and looked around. He rolled up the carpet and, with the bag over his shoulder, the carpet tucked under his arm and the stick in his hand, he strode off into the city.

The first person he met was an old woman. "Is this the city where Princess Maya lives?" he asked.

"Indeed it is," she said.

"And how can I find her?" he asked.

"Every evening," said the old woman, "the princess comes and sits upon the palace roof for one whole hour, and – *oh! such great wonder!* – she lights the city with her beauty."

So that evening the prince waited outside the palace, and at sunset a slender maiden came and sat upon the roof. She wore a sari of shimmering silk and on her forehead was a golden band, set with diamonds and pearls. It seemed as if a silvery radiance shone around her; in her presence, night became day.

The prince gazed upon the beautiful Princess Maya. He could not take his eyes off her. She truly was beyond compare.

At midnight, he held his bag and he said, "Bag! Give me a shawl of shimmering silk, the very match of Princess Maya's sari!" And in there – inside the bag – was a shawl of shimmering silk.

He unrolled his carpet, sat down, crossed his legs and said, "Carpet! Take me to Princess Maya!"

The carpet rose up until it was higher than the roofs and flew over the city until it reached the palace. Then it went straight through an open window and landed in Princess Maya's room.

The prince looked around and saw the beautiful princess, lying asleep in her bed.

Soft and silent as a cat, he stood up and gently placed the silk shawl beside the sleeping princess. And then – back on the carpet – and he was off!

The next evening the prince again stood outside the palace and gazed upon the beautiful princess. At midnight he said, "Bag! Give me a necklace of diamonds and pearls, the very match of Princess Maya's golden headband!" And there it was – a golden necklace set with diamonds and pearls.

Again, he unrolled his carpet, sat down, crossed his legs and said, "Carpet! Take me to Princess Maya!" And again, off he flew, right into her room. He placed the necklace beside the sleeping princess. Then – back on the carpet – and he was off!

On the third evening the same things happened. The prince stood outside and gazed upon the beautiful princess. At midnight he said, “Bag! Give me a golden ring set with the finest diamonds in the world!” And there it was – a splendid glittering ring.

Again he unrolled his carpet, sat down, crossed his legs and flew to the palace and into her room.

But this time he did not place the gift beside the sleeping princess. Instead

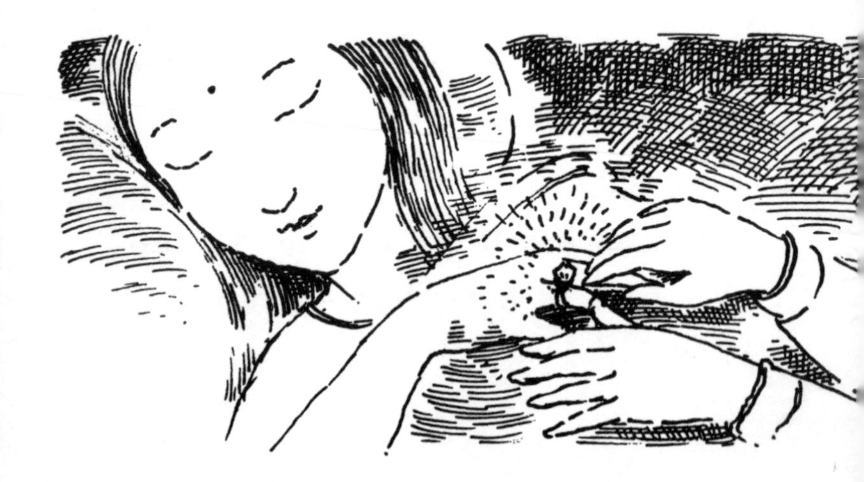

he lifted her hand and slipped the ring on one of her fingers.

Princess Maya stirred and opened her eyes. And when she saw the handsome young prince who held her hand, she said, "So, you are the one who gave me the shawl and the necklace and now this ring. Tell me, is there something you want, something I can give you in return?"

"There is," said the prince. "You yourself are the gift I seek, for you are the one I wish to marry."

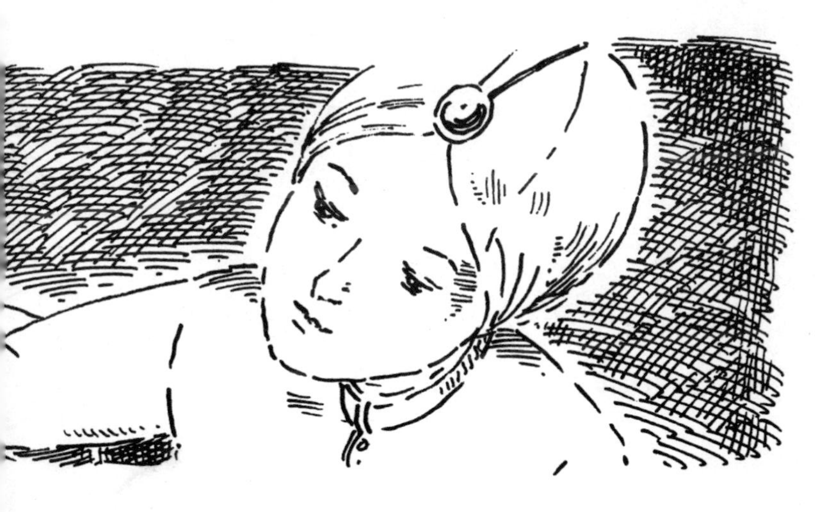

Princess Maya was surprised by the prince's words, but after they had talked together for much of the night she agreed to marry this handsome, generous young man. And in the morning she took him to her father, the raja of that land, and asked for his consent to their marriage.

But the raja said, "This man is a stranger. He came like a thief in the night. You cannot marry him."

The princess pleaded with her father until at last he agreed that if the prince could prove that he was a man of courage and strength, then she could marry him.

The raja said to the prince, "Outside the city there lives a fearsome ogre. He is as tall as two, as broad as three and has the strength of six. My people live in fear of him. Day in, day out, he comes and kills and steals. If you can capture this ogre, then you can marry my daughter."

The prince thought to himself, 'Capture an ogre? *This* is a task I can surely do!' And he set off with the stick in his hand.

He had not gone far when the mighty ogre saw him and came bounding towards him, roaring and bellowing in a great fury.

Then the prince said, "Stick! Do your work!" and the stick went flying through the air, and it beat the ogre until he fell helpless to the ground.

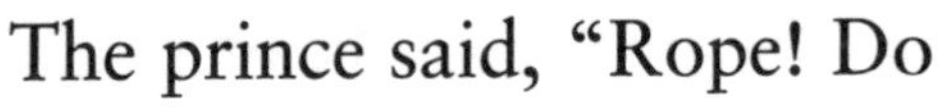

The prince said, "Rope! Do your work!" and the rope twirled itself off the stick and, quick as lightning, coiled itself round the ogre until he was bound, head to toe, so tight that he couldn't even move his little finger.

What then could the raja say? He had to agree to the marriage of the prince and his beautiful daughter, Princess Maya. So there was a wedding. And such a wedding! For a whole week there was feasting and rejoicing throughout the land.

At last the time came for the prince to return to his own land with his new bride. Then there was a long and magnificent procession: the prince and the princess and their attendants led the way, riding splendid black horses, and behind them trooped a hundred camels, bells jingling, all laden with treasures the raja had heaped upon them.

Now when the prince's horse had returned to the royal stables without a rider, his mother and father had been certain that their son was dead. So – imagine their happiness when he returned with his beautiful bride!

Well, the years passed, and the prince and beautiful Princess Maya lived together, happy and content. The prince always kept the bag, the stick and the carpet with him. And while the bag and the carpet were often useful, because his was a peaceful country and he had no enemies, he never again needed to use the stick.

An Indian tale

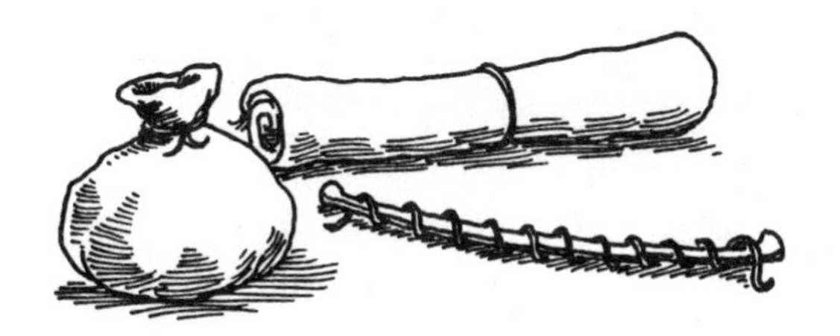

PEGASUS AND THE PROUD PRINCE

A Greek Tale

The ancient stories we call Greek myths were first written down over two and a half thousand years ago, but they probably go right back to even earlier times.

In Greek myths, the hero or heroine often has serious faults as well as good qualities. In *Pegasus and the Proud Prince,* Prince Bellerophon is brave and daring and, at first, humble enough to seek help from the goddess Athene. But he is also a show-off and thinks too much of himself. When he decides that he, a mortal, can visit the gods at their home on Mount Olympus, Zeus has to punish him. There is a proverb that sums up the message of Bellerophon's story: "Pride comes before a fall."

Some writers describe the Chimera as having a lion's head on a goat's body with a snake's tail. I chose the version where she has the heads of all three, because it seemed the most fantastic. She is, anyway, such an unlikely-looking creature that her name, *chimera*, is used in the English language to describe a wild, foolish dream or fancy.

THE FLYING CARPET

An Indian Tale

Kind deeds are almost always rewarded in magical tales, wherever they come from in the world. Because this is an Indian story, the bird whose life is spared is an exotic parrot. In European stories, the hero may save an eagle or a fish because these are creatures more commonly found in European countries.

One of the best known reward stories is *The Fisherman and his Wife* (a German tale found in most collections of *Grimms' Fairy Tales*). A kind fisherman throws a fish back in the sea to save it, despite his hunger and poverty. He is rewarded with wishes, but his greedy wife spoils everything by asking for too much. They both end up back where they started, still poor and hungry.

The prince in *The Flying Carpet,* like proud Bellerophon, sets off on a great adventure. They both fly through the air, defeat a fearsome creature and marry a princess. But the Indian Prince is wise and content with what he has. Unlike Prince Bellerophon and the fisherman's greedy wife, he lives happily ever after.

MAGICAL TALES *from* AROUND THE WORLD

Retold by Margaret Mayo ✳ *Illustrated by Peter Bailey*

PEGASUS AND THE PROUD PRINCE
and The Flying Carpet ISBN 1 84362 086 3 £3.99

UNANANA AND THE ENORMOUS ELEPHANT
and The Feathered Snake ISBN 1 84362 087 1 £3.99

THE FIERY PHOENIX
and The Lemon Princess ISBN 1 84362 088 X £3.99

THE GIANT SEA SERPENT
and The Unicorn ISBN 1 84362 089 8 £3.99

THE MAN-EATING MINOTAUR
and The Magic Fruit ISBN 1 84362 090 1 £3.99

THE MAGICAL MERMAID
and Kate Crackernuts ISBN 1 84362 091 X £3.99

THE INCREDIBLE THUNDERBIRD
and Baba Yaga Bony-legs ISBN 1 84362 092 8 £3.99

THE DARING DRAGON
and The Kingdom Under the Sea ISBN 1 84362 093 6 £3.99